The Hare and the TORTOISE

and other Fables of La Fontaine

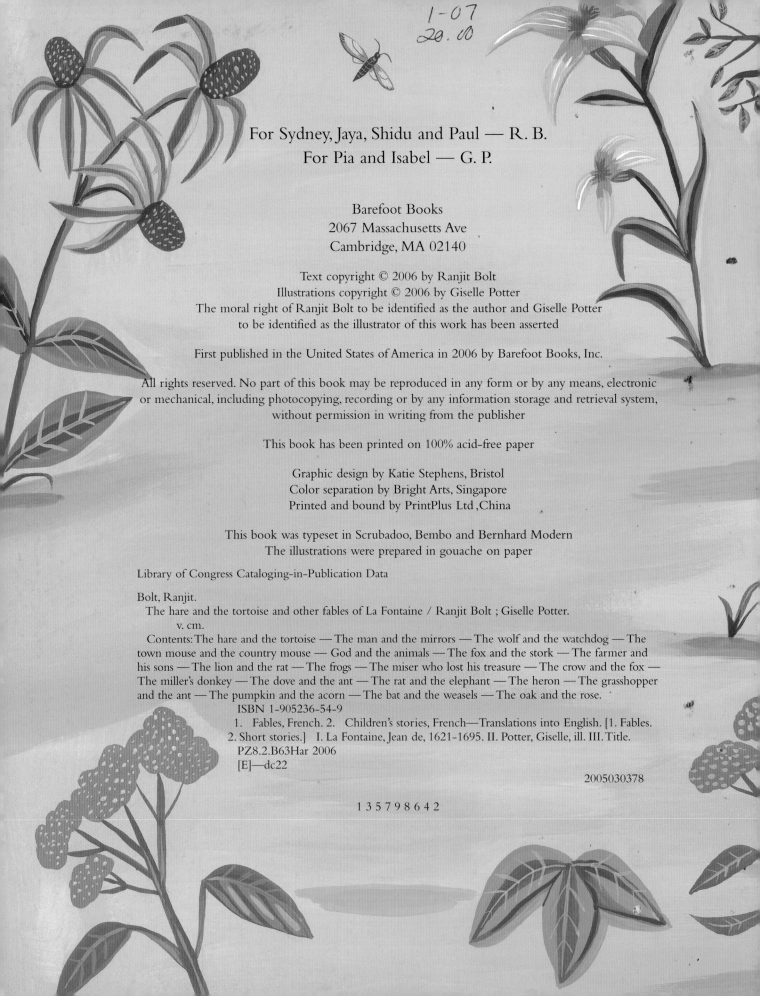

For Sydney, Jaya, Shidu and Paul — R. B.
For Pia and Isabel — G. P.

Barefoot Books
2067 Massachusetts Ave
Cambridge, MA 02140

First published in the United States of America in 2006 by Barefoot Books, Inc.

This book has been printed on 100% acid-free paper

Graphic design by Katie Stephens, Bristol
Color separation by Bright Arts, Singapore
Printed and bound by PrintPlus Ltd ,China

This book was typeset in Scrubadoo, Bembo and Bernhard Modern
The illustrations were prepared in gouache on paper

Library of Congress Cataloging-in-Publication Data

Bolt, Ranjit.
   The hare and the tortoise and other fables of La Fontaine / Ranjit Bolt ; Giselle Potter.
      v. cm.
   Contents: The hare and the tortoise — The man and the mirrors — The wolf and the watchdog — The
town mouse and the country mouse — God and the animals — The fox and the stork — The farmer and
his sons — The lion and the rat — The frogs — The miser who lost his treasure — The crow and the fox —
The miller's donkey — The dove and the ant — The rat and the elephant — The heron — The grasshopper
and the ant — The pumpkin and the acorn — The bat and the weasels — The oak and the rose.
      ISBN 1-905236-54-9
      1. Fables, French. 2. Children's stories, French—Translations into English. [1. Fables.
   2. Short stories.] I. La Fontaine, Jean de, 1621-1695. II. Potter, Giselle, ill. III. Title.
      PZ8.2.B63Har 2006
      [E]—dc22

                                                                                    2005030378

                        1 3 5 7 9 8 6 4 2

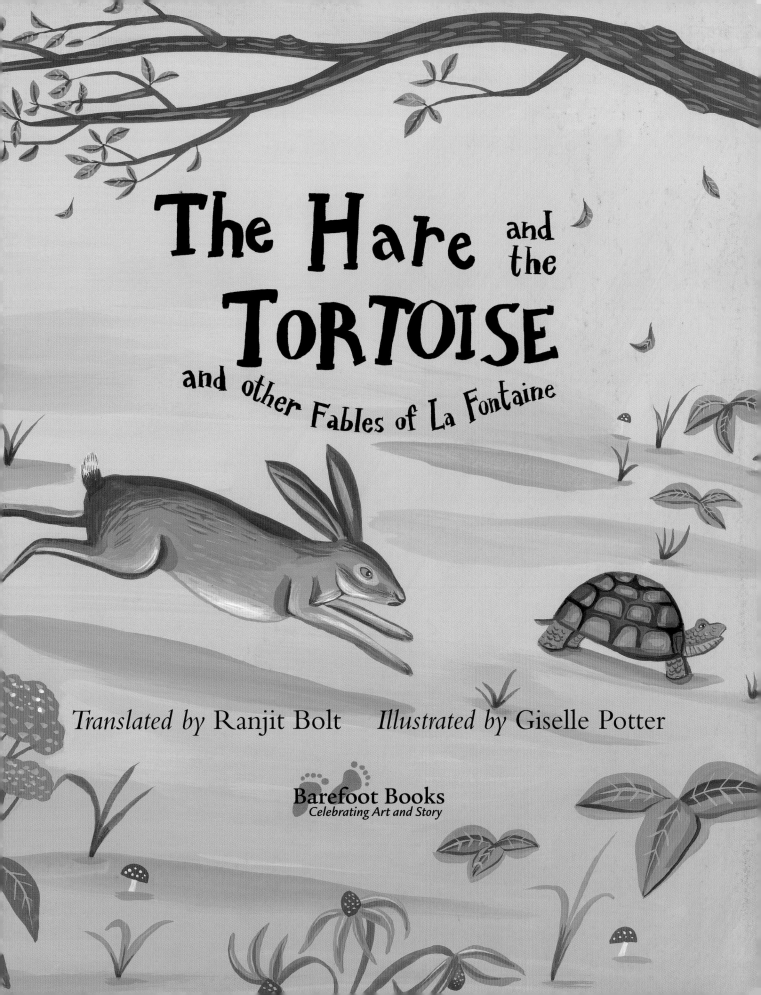

The Hare and the TORTOISE
and other Fables of La Fontaine

Translated by Ranjit Bolt   Illustrated by Giselle Potter

Barefoot Books
Celebrating Art and Story

Contents

Introduction

A fable is a kind of story. In fact, for the Romans the word "fabula" meant "story," and it's from this that "fabulous" comes. Fables usually have a moral, which means that they have something to say about what happens when we behave in certain ways. Often, the stories are quite funny and far-fetched, but their message always hits the mark.

Jean de La Fontaine (1621–95) was a French poet who is now best known for his *Fables*, which he wrote as a series of twelve books between 1668 and 1694. He did not make up the fables he wrote but adapted them from much, much older ones and presented them in clever, rhyming verse. Many of the fables on which he based his own were first written in Sanskrit, probably in Kashmir, northern India, in the fourth century AD. The collection was known as the *Panchatantra*. It was prepared for three young princes who had been behaving so badly that their father, the king, and all of their tutors became desperate. The king went to his wise vizier for help, and the vizier then wrote a series of animal fables, each with a hidden message. Their plan worked. Within a year, the three princes had understood the basic lessons about human conduct and leadership and were on their way to becoming wise rulers.

Two hundred years later, a Persian shah sent his physician, Burzoe, to India to find a herb that was said to give eternal life to whoever ate it. Burzoe did not return with the herb; instead he brought back the *Panchatantra* and translated it into Persian. The shah was so delighted with the fables that he kept the translation in a special shrine room in his palace. About three hundred years after that, when the Muslims had conquered Persia, a scholar named Ibn al-Mukaffa came across the stories. He translated them into Arabic and called the collection *Kalila Wa Dimna*. It was so popular that it soon became part of Muslim culture, and it was the Arabs who took the fables to Spain, where they were translated into Spanish in the early thirteenth century. They were first translated into French during the seventeenth century, and La Fontaine based his fables to some extent upon the French translation.

La Fontaine also drew on another major collection, Aesop's *Fables*. Not much is known about Aesop, but there is a theory that he was a tongue-tied Greek slave who lived in the sixth century BC and who was granted the power to speak and craft fables in return for his generosity to an attendant of the goddess Isis. Whoever he was and however he came to invent or adapt the fables, Aesop is the father of the fable tradition in the West. However, for the quality of his writing and the brilliance of his wit, La Fontaine has to be the king.

When they travel from country to country, century to century, and translator to translator, fables change in the process. I am happy to have joined such a long history of translators with this version of the fables, and I hope you enjoy reading them and choosing your favorites. Perhaps you will even make up some of your own!

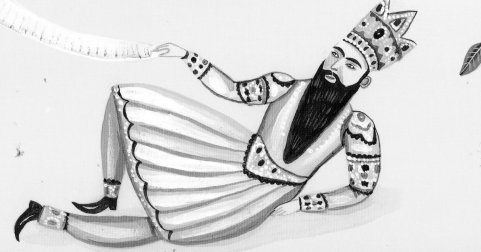

The Hare and the Tortoise

While being a brilliant runner's fine,

What *counts* is setting out on time.

I have a little tale to tell

That proves this point extremely well,

About a tortoise and a hare.

"You see that old tree over there,"

The tortoise said. "I'm betting you

I get to it before you do."

START

FINISH

"Before I do!" the hare replied,

And laughed until he almost died,

"Are you insane, for goodness sake!

How wild a bet can someone make?"

"I bet I *can*," the tortoise said.

They shook on it and went ahead.

The stakes were laid out by the tree.

(Don't ask me what those stakes might be,

Nor whom they chose as referee —

You always have one, though, at races.)

The hare could do it in four paces.

He could have got there and returned
In next to no time, but he spurned
A hollow victory, so instead,
While off the tortoise slowly sped,
He took a nap then ate some grass,
Tested the wind and let time pass.
The tortoise now was in top gear,
Doing at least a mile a year,
Which was as fast as she could go.
You should have heard her puff and blow,
But still the hare would not begin,
Still he despised an easy win.

He hummed a tune, did a headstand,

Anything *but* the task at hand.

Seeing the tortoise near the tree,

He did *hare off* eventually.

Fast as an arrow from a bow,

This burst of speed proved pointless, though —

Although it was a record run,

The tortoise had already won.

"What did I tell you?" she tee-hee'd.

"What use is your amazing speed?

I've won! I don't know where you'd be

If you'd a house to lug like me!"

FINISH

The Man and the Mirrors

There lived a man who was in love —
One person he adored above
All others, and that person was
None other than himself. Because
He thought he looked so very fine,
Though he saw mirrors all the time
That seemed to tell him otherwise.
He'd say, "It isn't me that lies,

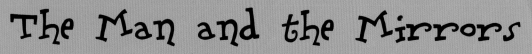

It's mirrors." All around the place
They'd let him see his ugly face —
In houses, shops and young men's pockets,
And certain sorts of ladies' lockets.
These mirrors caused him such dismay,
At last he hid himself away
In a far corner where he knew
No mirror would offend his view.
But in this wild secluded spot,
Though looking glasses there were not,

There was a river flowing near
Whose waters were extremely clear,
In which he sadly chanced to see
His face reflected perfectly.
Covered in anger and confusion,
He thought, "It must be an illusion.
From now on I'll avoid this stream
Although not coming here does seem
A pity — it's a pleasant place."

I have described this tragic case
Because we're all not far behind —
That man was like the human mind,
Which thinks, alas, quite naturally,
That it's as perfect as can be.
The mirrors stand for others who,
By being faulty through and through,
Show us that we are faulty too.
And for the stream, you needn't look
Beyond the stories in this book.

The Wolf and the Watchdog

The watchdogs kept the wolf away.

In fact, so good a job did they

That he was merely skin and bone.

One day he met, quite near his home,

A watchdog who was sleek and fat,

Stocky and stout, and strong at that.

So that the wolf, who had a hunch

The dog would make a first-class lunch,

Nevertheless did not attack,

But very prudently held back.

"Hello, sir dog," he humbly said.

"You do look handsome and well fed!"

"You could be looking this way too,"
The watchdog said, "it's up to you.
Just leave your hard life in the wood.
Can you not see that it's no good?
Scratching and scrabbling all the time,
And fighting for your meals, while I'm
As spoiled as any beast alive.
You can't imagine how I thrive,
Or rather, I can *show* you how,
If you would just come with me now."
"I'm very much obliged to you,"
Said wolf. "What would I have to do?"

"Practically nothing," said the dog.

"Easy as falling off a log.

Chase a few tramps and thieves away,

Join with the children in their play

And please your master, and you'll be

Stroked, hugged and kissed continually,

And given tasty things to eat,

Bones and delicious scraps of meat."

The wolf was dreaming of a bone.

He shed a tear, then set off home.

As he was going, he caught sight

Of something leathery and bright

'Round the dog's neck. "What's that?" said he.

"Oh, nothing that need bother me,"

The dog replied. "What is it, though?"
"Only my collar, don't you know,
For when they tie me up." "I see!
You mean to say you don't roam free?"
"Not always, no, not everywhere,"
The dog replied, "but I don't care."
"You should care," said the wolf. "For me
Life's worthless if you can't roam free
And that one thing's enough to beat
All of your bones and bits of meat!"
With that, the wolf went on his way,
Quite free, as he still is today.

The Town Mouse
and the Country Mouse

A town mouse asked a country mouse

Over one evening to his house.

They dined on lobster thermidor,

On oysters, and a whole roast boar,

Drank vintage wines with everything —

It was a meal fit for a king.

As they were gaily digging in,

They heard outside a fearful din.

Someone began to rant and roar

And crash and bang on the front door.

"I'm out of here!" the town mouse said,

And he immediately fled,

With his astonished guest in tow.

The racket stopped quite quickly, though,

And they came back. It might have been

A calm and quiet rural scene.

The town mouse said, "Let's try some roast."

"No thanks," the other told his host.

"I'm off. Tomorrow come to mine.

The supper won't be half so fine,

None of your town mouse luxuries,

But we'll be eating it in peace."

God and the Animals

God asked the animals one day

Whether each species felt OK.

He started with the elephant.

"So, is there anything you want?

Your tail has never really grown,

Your ears could do with trimming down . . . "

"I'm fine," replied the elephant,

"But I'm not sure about the ant.

She's such a tiny little beast,

Surely her size could be increased?"

The ant said, "No, I like my size,

It's quite sufficient in my eyes,

But have you thought about the whale?

He has no stupid ears or tail,

But goodness, is he big or what?
He could be shrunk by quite a lot."
God asked the slug about his slime.
The slug replied, "No, no, I'm fine.
I think the snake though, by the by,
Could do with being a bit less dry."
So every beast replied in turn —
It saw no reason for concern
About itself, but it could find
Some species of another kind
With things that needed sorting out.
We humans are without a doubt
The worst of creatures in this way.
We'll point out others' faults all day,
But when it comes to us, oh, no —
There's not one thing that needs to go!

The Fox and the Stork

When the fox entertained his friend,

The stork, he hadn't much to spend.

Indeed, he was so down-at-heel,

All he could manage for a meal

Was clear soup served up in a dish.

Now eating this was ticklish

For the poor stork, his long thin beak

Was not soup-friendly, so to speak.

He'd scarcely had a drop before
He found there wasn't any more —
His charming host had slurped it all.
The fox was riding for a fall,
And sure enough was made to pay
When the stork asked him back one day.
"It's quite short notice, but that's fine.
You're on," said fox. Come dinnertime
He duly visited the stork,
Who'd cooked some lamb — or was it pork? —

It smelled delicious anyway.

The eager fox exclaimed, "I say,

Dear stork, your cooking smells sublime,

I'll come and eat here any time!"

He was a-tremble with delight

For he'd a healthy appetite —

Of course he had, all foxes do —

And then the stork served up the stew.

Now, this was the revenge he got:

The stew was in a slender pot

That ended in a sort of spout,

Too narrow for the fox's snout

But out of which the stork's long beak

Could have got bits of meat all week.

The fox went hungry home to bed,

With drooping tail and hanging head.

He couldn't have been much more stricken

If he'd been stolen by a chicken.

My tale's for *you*, you tricky folk —

Be warned, before you trick a bloke.

You shouldn't dish it out if you

Aren't ready to receive it too.

The Farmer and his Sons

You cannot think what blessings lurk

Behind a bit of good hard work . . .

A farmer who owned lots of land,

Feeling his end was close at hand,

Summoned his sons to him and said,

"Well, fairly shortly I'll be dead,

And when I've passed away, perhaps

You'll want to sell our farm. But, chaps,

Pay heed now, 'cause before I go

There's something that you ought to know:

There's treasure buried on our land —

A crock of gold. D'you understand?

I'm not quite sure where it would be,

But dig about religiously

And you will find it, I'll be bound.

It's not too far beneath the ground.

Dig twice if need be, but dig well,

And sure as it is hot in hell

You'll find it. Mind you leave no spot
Undug, in case that's where the pot
Is hidden." Then he passed away,
And before dawn the following day,
The sons were out with spade and hoe
Digging the land up. To and fro
They went for weeks upturning ground.
There was no treasure to be found.

They dug for all that they were worth,

And not one coin did they unearth.

But goodness, they improved their fields.

The farm that year had record yields,

And brought them gold, not in a pot,

Not even buried, but so what?

Hard work's a treasure on its own,

As their wise father's trick had shown.

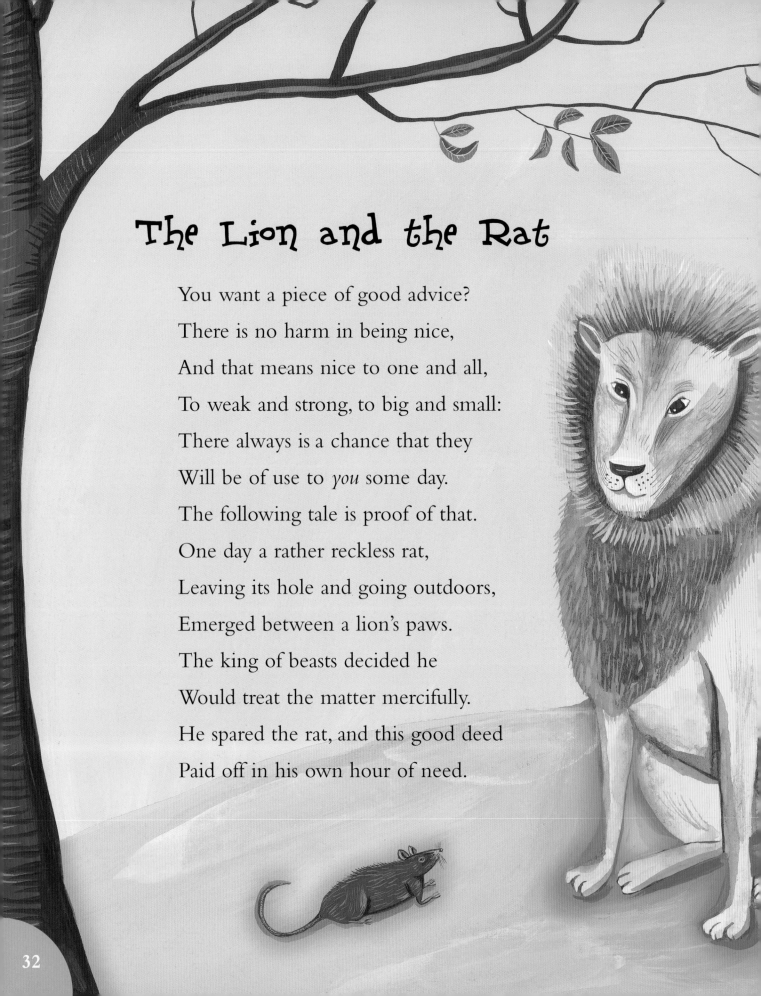

The Lion and the Rat

You want a piece of good advice?

There is no harm in being nice,

And that means nice to one and all,

To weak and strong, to big and small:

There always is a chance that they

Will be of use to *you* some day.

The following tale is proof of that.

One day a rather reckless rat,

Leaving its hole and going outdoors,

Emerged between a lion's paws.

The king of beasts decided he

Would treat the matter mercifully.

He spared the rat, and this good deed

Paid off in his own hour of need.

Who would have thought a mere rat would

Be placed to do a lion good?

But then the lion chanced to get

Caught in a big-game-hunter's net.

He roared and rolled and thrashed about,

But he could simply not get out,

And then the rat ran up and gnawed

The nasty squares of narrow cord

That made the net up, one by one,

Until enough had come undone

To make a spacious opening gape

Through which the lion could escape.

Which proves another point of course —

Time will accomplish more than force,

No matter though it take an age,

And quiet patience more than rage.

The Frogs

The frogs thought democratic rule

(Their current system) wasn't cool.

And so they asked Jove for a change,

Which he was willing to arrange.

He sent the frogs a king instead,

A sluggish one, as good as dead,

Who dropped upon them from on high,

Fell literally from the sky,

And landed with a splash so loud,

The frogs, who are a nervous crowd

As well as very silly, hid —

Dive deep into the pond they did,

And lurked in holes beneath the weeds,

Or mid the rushes and the reeds.

Each cowered in its hiding place,

Afraid of coming face to face

With what he thought must surely be

A giant, but was actually

A large and very heavy log.

Though terrified of it, one frog

Plucked up the guts to leave its nook

And take a timid, trembling look.

It crept up, though extremely scared.

Soon afterward a second dared

To follow it, and then a third . . .

Until a flock, if that's the word,

Had ventured up. The frogs grew bolder,

They hopped up on the log king's shoulder.

He let them perch there, and kept still.

But soon the frogs had had their fill

And once again complained to Jove.

"Our monarch doesn't even move!"

They whined, so Jove gave in again

And sent a moving king — a crane

That liked to kill and crunch and munch

Ten frogs with tea and ten for lunch.

The frogs complained to Jove once more.

"Whatever you folk ask me for

I have to give you, is that it?"

He answered them. "Well, wait a bit.

You should have kept the government

You started with, and been content.

And failing that, the second one

Was better by a mile than none.

I wouldn't ask to change again,

There's plenty worse things than a crane.

Instead of hating what you've got,

Try and be happy with your lot."

The Miser Who Lost His Treasure

Rich men should know what money's for,

Or else they may as well be poor . . .

A miser heaped up tons of gold,

More than his treasure chest could hold.

But did he spend his pile? Oh, no —

He hoarded it. It was as though

He thought he'd one day live again,

And meant to spend his money then.

He'd fret about security —

Was it as safe as it could be,

This hoard of his? It drove him mad.

In fact the worry got so bad

That in the end he hid the lot

In a big hole, in a safe spot.

His mind was buried with his gold,

Which seemed to have a stranglehold

Upon his thoughts. Ten times a day

He'd scurry back to where it lay

To check that everything was fine,

Or whether there was any sign

Of interference with the spot,

And laughed for joy when there was not.

His neighbor watched him scan the ground.

"He's buried loot there I'll be bound,"

He thought. He went and dug that night,

Took all the gold and then sat tight.

No sooner had the miser seen

A big hole where his gold had been

Than how the wretched fellow cried!

He wept and wailed, he groaned and sighed,

And beat his breast and tore his hair,

And wallowed in complete despair.

The gardener, seeing this display,

Asked what had caused so much dismay.

"My gold!" the miser howled. "It's gone!
It's been made off with by someone!"
"What did you hide it out here for?
You bury gold in time of war.
A chest's far better, and with that
Your money's easier to get at."
"Get at?! You think my gold's to spend?
You must be raving mad, my friend!
Once money's spent it's gone, for good!"
"Then why in such a tragic mood?
What have you lost?" the gardener said.
"Bury a stone there now instead —
It's worth as much as gold to you!"
So now the wretched miser knew.

The Crow and the Fox

Perched way up high among the trees,

Sir Crow held in his beak a cheese.

Sir Fox picked up the cheese's scent,

And came with hungry, mean intent

Toward Sir Crow, whom he addressed,

"*Lord* Crow, your plumage is the best

I've ever seen. You must rejoice

In such fine feathers. If your *voice*

Can only match them, you've no peer,

You are the finest bird 'round here . . ."

Thrilled by these flattering words, Sir Crow

Felt a tremendous urge to show

Sir Fox how well he sang, and so
Opened his beak and dropped the cheese,
On which Sir Fox was quick to seize.
"Sir Crow," he said, "from this perhaps
You'll learn how flatterers set their traps —
Heeding their speeches doesn't pay.
They only flatter you when they
Are after something that you've got.
I've warned you, and I tell you what,
My warning's worth a cheese, so there!"
At this, Sir Crow was in despair,
And of his folly far from proud —
He'd learned his lesson and he vowed
Never again to heed a word
Of flattery from beast or bird.

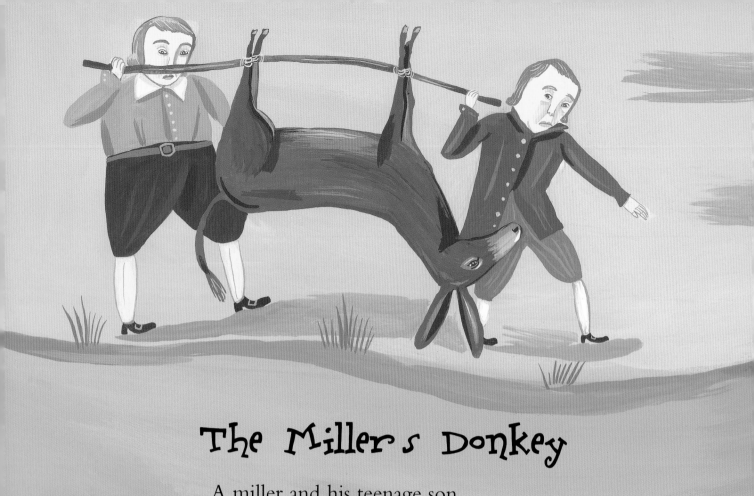

The Miller's Donkey

A miller and his teenage son,

A big strong lad who weighed a ton,

Were going to the local fair.

They planned to sell their donkey there.

So it would not arrive dead beat,

They'd tied the donkey by its feet

To a pole, and were carrying it,

Quite like a porker on a spit.

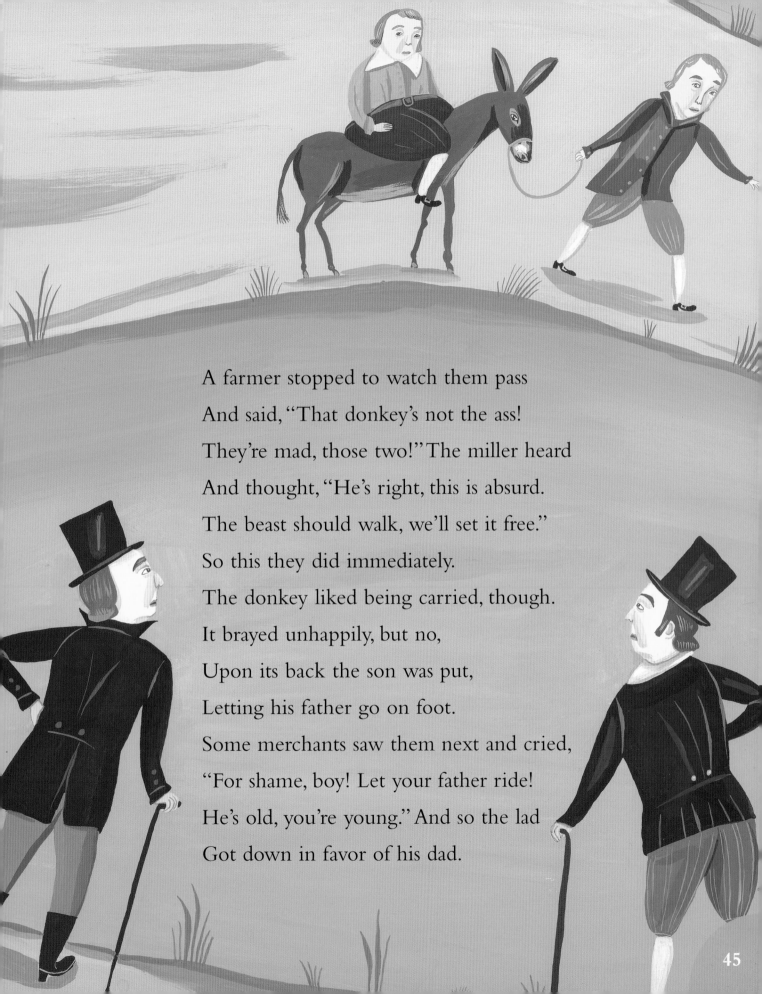

A farmer stopped to watch them pass

And said, "That donkey's not the ass!

They're mad, those two!" The miller heard

And thought, "He's right, this is absurd.

The beast should walk, we'll set it free."

So this they did immediately.

The donkey liked being carried, though.

It brayed unhappily, but no,

Upon its back the son was put,

Letting his father go on foot.

Some merchants saw them next and cried,

"For shame, boy! Let your father ride!

He's old, you're young." And so the lad

Got down in favor of his dad.

Some girls next spotted them. Said one,
"Look how that old man treats his son.
He makes the poor boy walk while he's
All comfortable and takes his ease!"
"Mind your own business!" yelled the miller,
But the girls' comments just got shriller.
So in the end he let his son
Get up behind and they rode on,
Both mounted now. They'd scarcely gone
Ten yards before another group
Cried, "Hey, you daft old nincompoop!
That's not how decent folk behave!
You'll grind that beast into its grave!

Poor creature! Look! It's fit to drop!"

So yet again they had to stop.

They both got off and walked this time.

"Well, really, what a pantomime!"

Remarked the person they next met.

"Your donkey's in fine fettle, yet

You're both on foot! You're off your head!"

"What if I am?' the miller said.

"You can't please all the world at once;

The wise man just does what he wants."

With which the pair just walked on past.

They'd learned their lesson at long last.

The Dove and the Ant

I told you several pages back

That if you take a pleasant tack

With people it will often pay.

This story also ends that way —

The moral's more or less the same.

One day a certain ringdove came

To a clear rivulet to drink.

As she was bending o'er the brink,

An ant fell in. He strove in vain

To reach the bank, or shore, again —

I say "or shore" because to him

It was an ocean he was in.

The dove, to save him from this pass,

Kindly threw in a blade of grass,

48

And on this island or this spit
The ant soon found it safe to sit.
He thereby reached dry land at last.
A barefoot peasant now came past
Who had a crossbow in his hand.
He saw the ringdove drinking and
Pictured her on a supper platter.
He had just aimed his crossbow at her
When the ant nipped him on the toe.
This being bare, he yelped, and so
The bird, alerted by his cry,
Launched herself high into the sky.
With her his supper, too, took flight —
No pigeon stew for *him* tonight.

The Rat and the Elephant

A rat, as small as you could want,
Happened to spy an elephant,
A mighty beast of massive frame.
But the rat mocked him all the same,
By passing comments on his gait,
Which was exceedingly sedate.
In fact was practically as slow
As it is possible to go
Without completely standing still.
He was the size of a small hill
And on him rode, in several tiers,
A prince, his courtiers, his viziers,
His wives, his children, folk like that,
A dog, a monkey and a cat.

The elephant carried this huge weight

As lightly as a dinner plate.

People looked on, as he passed by,

Exclaiming "Gosh!" and "Cool!" and "My!"

The rat, meanwhile, could not see why

An elephant inspired such awe.

"What are you gaping at him for?

Because he is so big and tall?

What if he is? I may be small,

Compact of body and of limb,

But I am just as good as him."

Thus, angrily, remarked the rat.

He would have said more, but the cat

Suddenly pouncing from above

Snaffled him up, as if to prove

That, even though he rave and rant,

A rat is *not* an elephant.

The Heron

Being fussy isn't good for you,

It's better if you can make do

With whatever comes along.

Just read this if you think I'm wrong . . .

A heron came across a stream

Whose waters were so very clean

He could see through them just like glass

And watch whatever fish might pass.

He saw a carp and then a pike —

They swam as coolly as you like

Right near the bank on which he stood.

Either of these two fish he could

With ease have caught in his long beak

And they'd have fed him for a week.

But he was not yet hungry, so,

Nice though they looked, he let them go.

But soon he found that time had flown

And that his appetite had grown.

So near the water's edge he drew
And saw a bream go by. This too
He wouldn't touch. "I don't like bream,
There's better fishing in this stream.
A humble bream could never be
A fit meal for a bird like me.
I'll wait a while and play it cool."
So wait he did, the silly fool.
A gudgeon next came swimming by.
"Eat gudgeon? Yuck! I'd rather die!
It's not worth opening my beak
For such a microscopic freak!"
The haughty heron spoke too soon.

Morning went by, and afternoon,
And not another fish swam past.
He got so hungry that at last
He gobbled up a water snail.
Children, be wise and heed my tale.
Take what life offers and be glad.
I'm sure that heron wished he had.

The Grasshopper and the Ant

The grasshopper had sung his song

All the delightful summer long

Instead of gathering in supplies.

Now only did he realize,

With winter coming on, that he

Could not have supper, lunch or tea!

He couldn't find a scrap of food,

The cupboards in his larder showed

Not even one small worm or fly.

He'd had it, he was high and dry.

He went to see his neighbor ant

And told her of his sudden want —

"Give me a bit of food," he said,
"Or you'll be sorry when I'm dead!
Please . . . just enough to last 'til spring,
This isn't really borrowing —
By August you shall be repaid,
With interest." Ants are all afraid
Of lending, and the one found here
Shared with her nation that strange fear
(Which can in some respects be wrong).
"What did you *do* all summer long?"
She asked the would–be borrower.
"I sang my song," he answered her,
"To passersby, all night and day."
"You simply sang your song, you say?
Well done! I cannot fault you there . . .
Now you can dance, for all I care."

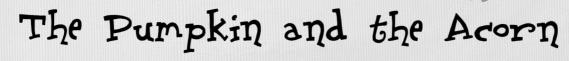

The Pumpkin and the Acorn

God has arranged things very well

As in an instant you can tell

By looking at the world. Indeed

A pumpkin's all the proof you need.

A peasant thought the way that God

Had made the world was rather odd.

"He's made mistakes, a lot of them —

Look at the pumpkin's long thin stem.

It isn't strong enough to take

So great a weight for goodness sake!

A pumpkin should be on a tree,

Yes, something like an *oak* would be

The perfect place for it. Instead

It has a thin stalk, like I said,

While on the oak God goes and puts

Acorns as small as hazelnuts!

They should have left it all to me.
I'd have arranged things differently,
And better, or I'll eat my hat.
To hang a tiny thing like that
On such a massive tree! It's mad!"
A few days later this same lad
Was snoozing underneath an oak
When, with a sharp jolt, he awoke —
An acorn had dropped off the tree
And struck him very painfully
Right on his nose, which stung and bled.
"That was a nasty blow!" he said,
"And from an acorn! Just suppose
That what had landed on my nose
Had been a heavier object — say
A pumpkin! It's as plain as day
I've got the world completely wrong;
God made it just right all along."

The Bat and the Weasels

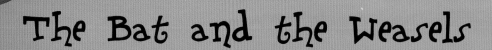

One day a rather scatty bat,

Who scarcely knew what he was at,

Flew straight into a weasel's nest.

This sudden, uninvited guest

Annoyed the weasel quite a bit.

"You horrid beast! Get out of it!

How dare you come into my home?

Of all the enemies I've known

Rats are the worst, and you're a rat,

You needn't try denying that."

And promptly pouncing on him, she

Prepared to eat him with her tea.

"What? Me? A rat? Who told you so?"

Replied the desperate bat. "Why, no!

A rat indeed! But how absurd!

Isn't it obvious I'm a bird?

Do rats have wings? Well look at these.

See? I'm a bird! Don't eat me! PLEASE!"

The weasel was convinced, and so
She put him down and let him go.
Before the week had reached its end,
Would you believe, our batty friend
Had found his way, the little pest,
Into *another* weasel's nest.
"A bird!" she cried. "Well, what a treat!
Birds are my favorite things to eat."
And up she caught him in her snout.
"No, wait!" the bat now shouted out,
"I'm NOT a bird. You can't eat ME!
It's plain for anyone to see
That I am just a common rat.
I hope to God you're not a cat . . ."
So, by a very narrow squeak,
And for the second time that week,
The bat escaped with life and limb.
We'd all do well to copy him
And change our ways to suit the whim
Of those whose company we're in.

The Oak and the Rose

You'll find it's better in the end

Not to be stubborn, but to bend . . .

The oak tree used to mock the rose:

"The smallest little breeze that blows

Is like a storm to you, my friend.

Oh, how I laugh to see you bend

While I stand firm, am stout and strong.

A storm could blow on all day long
And still I wouldn't bend one jot,
But stand here, rooted to the spot.
Not moving by a millimeter
To right or left; I could defeat a
Typhoon, so strongly am I grown
While you are buffeted and blown
To left and right by winds that *I*
Can't *feel*, still less be shaken by!"

No sooner had he said this than

On the horizon there began

To rise a wind, a whirling one,

A typhoon or a hurricane.

Soon it was blowing 'round the oak

And 'round the rose. It was no joke,

This storm, and the rose bent like mad,

Used all the suppleness it had

To stop itself being snapped in two.

The oak tree did what oak trees do:

It fought the storm with all its might,

Determined it should stay upright.

Its strength, though massive, was of course

Not equal to the typhoon's force,

And soon this mightiest of trees

Was toppled, rooted up with ease

Then blown quite casually away . . .

The bendy rose still bends today.

Afterword

Unless you read this book again,

Then that's your lot of La Fontaine,

But if you're sensibly inclined

You'll keep these stories in your mind.

Try not to copy that poor crow

Who let his lump of cheddar go,

Or the imprudent grasshopper,

But, seeing what fools those creatures were,

Be like the wise old ant instead,

Who through the summer used her head

And in the winter thus was able

Still to put dinner on the table.

Do this, child, and your future life

Will have more joy in it than strife,

A lot less tears, with luck, than laughter,

And end up happy ever after.

Barefoot Books
Celebrating Art and Story

At Barefoot Books, we celebrate art and story that opens
the hearts and minds of children from all walks of life, inspiring
them to read deeper, search further, and explore their own creative gifts.
Taking our inspiration from many different cultures, we focus on themes that
encourage independence of spirit, enthusiasm for learning, and sharing of
the world's diversity. Interactive, playful and beautiful, our products
combine the best of the present with the best of the past to
educate our children as the caretakers of tomorrow.

www.barefootbooks.com